TODAY'S 12 HOTTEST
MLB SUPERSTARS

by Tom Robinson

12 STORY LIBRARY

www.12StoryLibrary.com

12-Story Library is an imprint of Peterson Publishing Company and Press Room Editions.

Produced for 12-Story Library by Red Line Editorial

Photographs ©: Gene J. Puskar/AP images, cover, 1, 17; Photo Works/Shutterstock Images, 5, 7, 14–15, 26; Rena Schild/Shutterstock Images, 8, 12, 13; Stephen Brashear/AP Images, 9, 28; Kyodo/AP Images, 11; Richard Paul Kane/Shutterstock Images, 16; Chris O'Meara/ AP Images, 19; Kathy Willens/AP Images, 21; Cal Sport Media/AP Images, 22, 29; Mark J. Terrill/AP Images, 23; Michael Dwyer/AP Images, 25; Jeff Smith/Shutterstock Images, 27

ISBN
978-1-63235-018-3 (hardcover)
978-1-63235-078-7 (paperback)
978-1-62143-059-9 (hosted ebook)

Library of Congress Control Number: 2014946799

Printed in the United States of America
Mankato, MN
December, 2014

Go beyond the book. Get free, up-to-date content on this topic at 12StoryLibrary.com.

TABLE OF CONTENTS

MADISON BUMGARNER NAMED 2014 WORLD SERIES MVP

Madison Bumgarner was already established as a clutch pitcher in 2014. Then the 25-year-old left-hander turned in one of the best performances in World Series history. Bumgarner was the Most Valuable Player (MVP) of the 2014 World Series win against the Kansas City Royals. He won Game 1 with a strong effort. Then he threw a complete-game shutout in Game 5. Soon people began talking about whether Bumgarner could help the Giants by pitching an inning or two in Game 7. But he did much more than that. He pitched the final five innings of Game 7, preserving a 3-2 lead the entire time, to clinch San Francisco's third World Series in five years.

In three world championship runs, Bumgarner was the winning pitcher

1

The number of runs Bumgarner allowed in 21 innings pitched in the 2014 World Series.

Birth date: August 1, 1989
Birthplace: Hickory, North Carolina
Height: 6 feet 5 (1.96 m)
Weight: 235 pounds (107 kg)
Team: San Francisco Giants, 2009–
Breakthrough Season: Won 13 games in 2010, then pitched eight scoreless innings in Game 4 as San Francisco won its first World Series against the Texas Rangers
Awards: 2014 World Series MVP

in seven postseason games. And his performance in Game 7 of the 2014 series was the longest save in World Series history.

In his younger days, Bumgarner led South Caldwell High School of Hudson, North Carolina, to two straight state championship games. He was named the state's Gatorade High School Player of the Year as a senior pitcher, and he hit a game-clinching,

BEST ERA

Through 2014, Bumgarner had the best career World Series earned run average (ERA) of any pitcher in Major League Baseball (MLB) history with at least 25 innings. He allowed just one earned run in 36 World Series innings for a 0.25 ERA. Before Bumgarner, Jack Billingham held the record with a 0.36 ERA for the Cincinnati Reds between 1972 and 1976.

walk-off home run in the state final. The Giants took Bumgarner with the tenth pick of the 2007 draft. He made it to the big leagues two years later.

Bumgarner pitches in 2011.

MIGUEL CABRERA WINS THE TRIPLE CROWN

Miguel Cabrera has had a bat in his hand since his youngest days. He grew up in a family of baseball and softball players. He even lived next to a ballpark. Cabrera began his minor league baseball career as a shortstop. He was called up by the Florida Marlins in 2003. As a rookie, he played left field and third base. He has also been a right fielder, first baseman, and designated hitter.

Cabrera can do it all. He has a Triple Crown to prove it. That means he led his league in home runs, runs batted in (RBI), and batting average in the same year. Cabrera led the American League (AL) in each in 2012. He hit 44 home runs. He drove in 139 runs. His batting average was .330. The Triple Crown shows Cabrera is a skilled hitter. He gets on base often. His hits are also powerful and timely.

Cabrera has always produced as a hitter. In each of his first 11 seasons, he received votes for the league's MVP. Cabrera was the AL MVP as a member of the Detroit Tigers in 2012 and again in 2013.

CABRERA'S FIRST WALK-OFF

Cabrera had a special finish to his first major league game in 2003. He hit a home run to win the game for his team. He became the third player since 1900 to hit a walk-off home run in his first major-league game.

Cabrera prepares to swing during a 2011 game.

44

Number of home runs Cabrera hit in 2012.

Birth Date: April 18, 1983

Birthplace: Maracay, Venezuela

Teams: Florida Marlins, 2003–07; Detroit Tigers, 2008–

Height: 6 feet 4 (1.93 m)

Weight: 240 pounds (109 kg)

Breakthrough Season: Won the World Series with the Florida Marlins as rookie in 2003

Awards: AL MVP, 2012 and 2013

ROBINSON CANO LIVES UP TO HIS NAME

Former major league pitcher Jose Cano chose to honor one of baseball's great historical figures when his son was born in 1982. Robinson Cano was named after Jackie Robinson, the first black MLB player.

Cano played for the New York Yankees from 2005 to 2013.

Jose Cano honored the past. And perhaps he saw the future. Jackie Robinson was a very talented second baseman with

Cano tags out the Baltimore Orioles' David Lough at second base in 2014.

3

Number of errors Cano made in 2010 when he led the AL second basemen in fielding percentage.

Birth Date: October 22, 1982

Birthplace: San Pedro de Macoris, Dominican Republic

Teams: New York Yankees, 2005–13; Seattle Mariners, 2014–

Height: 6 feet (1.83 m)

Weight: 210 pounds (95 kg)

Breakthrough Season: Finished second in AL Rookie of the Year voting after joining the Yankees early in 2005 season

Awards: AL Gold Glove, 2010 and 2012; MVP of World Baseball Classic, 2013

the Brooklyn Dodgers. Robinson Cano would one day establish himself as one of baseball's best second basemen with the New York Yankees.

Cano learned baseball while growing up in the Dominican Republic. He signed with the Yankees when he was 18 years old. In nine seasons with the Yankees, Cano won the Silver Slugger Award for best offensive player at his position five times. He has been selected for the All-Star Game six times and won the Gold Glove as the AL's best defensive second baseman twice through 2014. Cano ranked in the top six in AL MVP voting four times with the Yankees. In 2014, Cano signed a 10-year $240 million contract with the Seattle Mariners.

4

YU DARVISH STARS ALL AROUND THE WORLD

Yu Darvish was familiar with American baseball before ever coming to the United States. MLB teams scouted him while he grew up playing in Japan. Darvish proved to be the best pitcher in his country. He starred on the Japanese national team. He pitched in the 2008 Beijing Olympics. He was then the winning pitcher in the championship game of the 2009 World Baseball Classic.

Darvish found similar success in the MLB. He joined the Texas Rangers in 2012. He finished third in the AL Rookie of the Year voting in 2012. A year later, he was second in voting for the AL Cy Young Award as the league's top pitcher.

Darvish throws hard. He also has many different pitches, throwing at different speeds and angles. Darvish used this skill to strike out 498 batters in his first two MLB seasons.

277

The number of batters Darvish struck out when he led MLB in that category in 2013.

Birth Date: August 16, 1986
Birthplace: Habikino, Osaka, Japan
Team: Texas Rangers, 2012–
Height: 6 feet 5 (1.96 m)
Weight: 215 pounds (98 kg)
Breakthrough Season: Made the All-Star Game as a rookie in 2012, his first season after leaving Japan
Awards: AL Rookie of the Month, April 2012

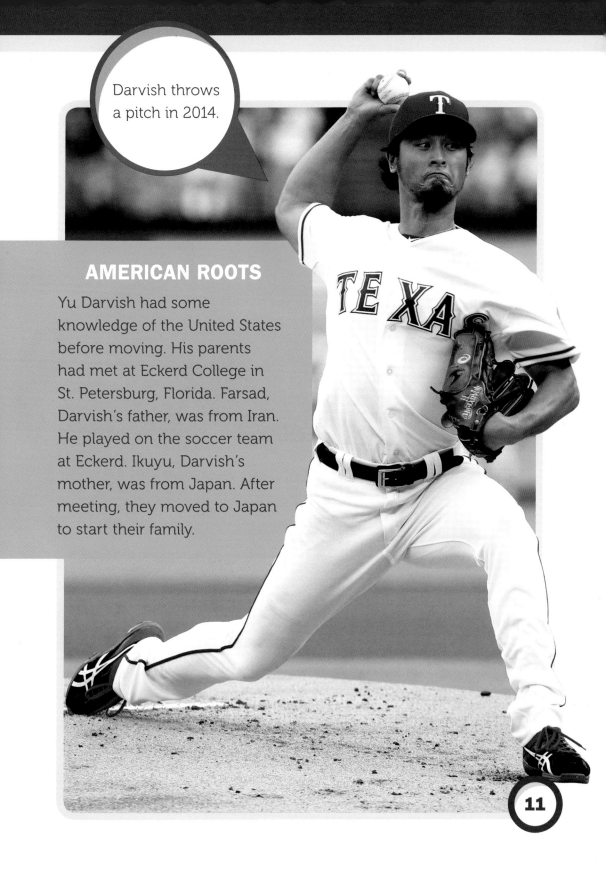

Darvish throws a pitch in 2014.

AMERICAN ROOTS

Yu Darvish had some knowledge of the United States before moving. His parents had met at Eckerd College in St. Petersburg, Florida. Farsad, Darvish's father, was from Iran. He played on the soccer team at Eckerd. Ikuyu, Darvish's mother, was from Japan. After meeting, they moved to Japan to start their family.

BRYCE HARPER BECOMES TEEN ALL-STAR

Bryce Harper hurried to the MLB. He rose to the top in a hurry, too. Harper started dreaming about becoming an MLB star when he was seven years old. After his sophomore year of high school, Harper wanted to speed up the process. Rather than graduate with his class, he earned his degree by passing a test called a GED. This allowed him to start college that fall. Harper was then eligible to be selected in the MLB Draft the next spring. Harper played one season of junior college baseball at Southern Nevada. Scouts saw that Harper had all five tools. He could run, throw, field, hit for average, and hit for power. He was picked first overall by the Washington Nationals in the 2010 draft.

Harper became the youngest non-pitcher ever selected to play in the All-Star Game in 2012.

OTHER TEENAGE STARS

Only two other teenagers were selected as All-Stars before Harper made it in 2012. Cleveland's Bob Feller made the AL team in 1938 but did not play. Dwight Gooden of the New York Mets pitched for the NL in 1984.

Harper played one year in the minor leagues. That year he switched from catcher to outfielder. This switch in positions was designed to keep him healthy. Catchers take a beating behind the plate. The Nationals wanted to protect their young star. Harper joined the Washington Nationals early in the 2012 season. Within months, he was a National League (NL) All-Star.

19

Harper's age when he was selected to play in the 2012 All-Star Game.

Birth Date: October 16, 1992

Birthplace: Las Vegas, Nevada

Team: Washington Nationals, 2012–

Height: 6 feet 3 (1.91 m)

Weight: 225 pounds (102 kg)

Breakthrough Season: Hit 22 home runs as a rookie in 2012

Awards: NL Rookie of the Year, 2012

Harper up to bat in 2012

CLAYTON KERSHAW BLOWS HITTERS AWAY

Kershaw uncoils his lanky frame to deliver a pitch in 2010.

Clayton Kershaw had the game of his life on June 18, 2014. That night he struck out 15 Colorado Rockies batters while throwing a no-hitter. Experts debated whether it was the best pitching performance ever.

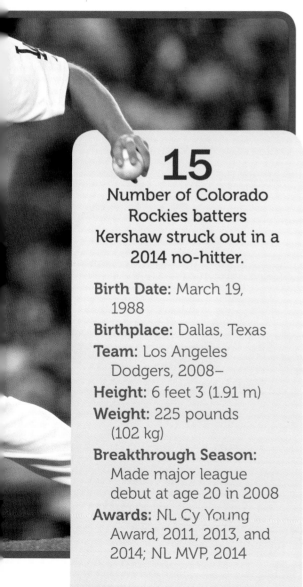

15

Number of Colorado Rockies batters Kershaw struck out in a 2014 no-hitter.

Birth Date: March 19, 1988
Birthplace: Dallas, Texas
Team: Los Angeles Dodgers, 2008–
Height: 6 feet 3 (1.91 m)
Weight: 225 pounds (102 kg)
Breakthrough Season: Made major league debut at age 20 in 2008
Awards: NL Cy Young Award, 2011, 2013, and 2014; NL MVP, 2014

Kershaw was the first pitcher in MLB history to strike out 15 batters without allowing a hit or walk.

Kershaw had grown used to dominating hitters. He was the nation's top high school player in 2006. He struck out all 15 batters he faced in a 2006 playoff game in Texas.

Kershaw joined the Los Angeles Dodgers in 2008. He continued dominating in his pro career. He was just 20 years old, making him the youngest player in the major leagues at the time. Just three years later, Kershaw led the NL in wins, earned run average, and strikeouts. This feat is called the pitching Triple Crown. Kershaw won the NL Cy Young Award as the league's top pitcher in 2011, 2013, and 2014. He was second in voting in 2012. He had the league's best ERA in all four seasons. And he was named the NL MVP in 2014. He was only the eleventh pitcher ever to win both the Cy Young and MVP awards in the same season.

ANDREW McCUTCHEN LEADS THE PIRATES TO THE PLAYOFFS

Andrew McCutchen's athletic abilities were evident from an early age. He played varsity baseball as an eighth grader. He led his county with a .591 average. He also excelled in football and track. But McCutchen was headed for pro baseball. The Pittsburgh Pirates selected him in the first round of the 2005 MLB Draft, just after he had finished high school.

In the minor leagues, McCutchen kept showing signs of what was ahead. In 2006 he was one of the top players in the Pirates' minor league system.

McCutchen connects on a pitch against the Cincinnati Reds in 2009.

194

McCutchen's NL-best number of hits in 2012.

Birth Date: October 10, 1986

Birthplace: Fort Meade, Florida

Team: Pittsburgh Pirates, 2009–

Height: 5 feet 10 (1.78 m)

Weight: 190 pounds (86 kg)

Breakthrough Season: Second in the NL in batting average at .327 in 2012

Awards: NL Gold Glove, 2012; NL MVP, 2013

McCutchen uses his speed to track down fly balls.

He made it to the major leagues three years later. On the fifth day of his big-league career, he had a four-hit game with two triples.

The Pittsburgh Pirates had been stuck. They had not had a winning season or been to the playoffs since 1992. That did not stop their young star center fielder, McCutchen, from committing to the team with a new contract in 2012.

The move paid off for McCutchen and the Pirates. In 2013, McCutchen helped break their losing streak and led the team to the playoffs. McCutchen used his speed to get and take away hits. He became the face of the Pirates. McCutchen was recognized for his role in the team's revival. He was named NL MVP in 2013.

DAVID ORTIZ SHINES WITH THE BAT

David Ortiz grew up around baseball. His father, Enrique, played professionally in the Dominican Republic. David was just 17 when he signed his first professional contract. Since then, Ortiz has proved it is not necessary to play the field to be a valuable baseball player. Ortiz has served as designated hitter for nearly 83 percent of the games in his major league career. As the designated hitter, he only bats.

Ortiz served this role exceptionally well for more than a decade in Boston. He finished in the top five in AL MVP voting for each of his first five seasons with the Red Sox. The team won the World Series twice during that time.

Ortiz is nicknamed "Big Papi" for his large size. He became a popular leader in Boston. The Red Sox had not won the World Series since 1918

54

Ortiz's career-high home run total in 2006.

Birth Date: November 18, 1975

Birthplace: Santo Domingo, Dominican Republic

Teams: Minnesota Twins, 1997–2002; Boston Red Sox, 2003–

Height: 6 feet 4 (1.93 m)

Weight: 230 pounds (104 kg)

Breakthrough Season: Hit 41 regular-season home runs for Boston in 2004, then hit five home runs and drove in 19 runs in 14 postseason games to lead the Red Sox to their first World Series title since 1918

Awards: AL Championship Series MVP, 2004; World Series MVP, 2013

before Ortiz joined the team. They won three in the next 11 seasons. One of these wins was in 2013. During the World Series, Ortiz batted .688 with two home runs against the St. Louis Cardinals. He was named World Series MVP.

Ortiz is known for steady in-season production and clutch playoff performances. The nine-time all-star holds almost every career record for designated hitters, including hits and home runs. He hit five home runs in the 2004 postseason, then did it again in 2013.

Ortiz watches the ball after hitting a home run against the Tampa Bay Rays in 2014.

BUSTER POSEY OVERCOMES INJURY

Gerald "Buster" Posey III played football, soccer, and basketball while growing up in Georgia. But he made a name for himself in baseball. While still in high school, Posey played internationally for the US Junior Olympic team.

Posey once played all nine fielding positions in a college baseball game for Florida State. He switched his regular position from shortstop to catcher between his freshman and sophomore seasons. As a junior, he was named the best college baseball player in the country. The San Francisco Giants made him the fifth overall pick in the 2008 MLB Draft.

Posey made it to the big leagues in late 2009. He had an immediate impact with the Giants. He was named NL Rookie of the Year in 2010. He also helped San Francisco win its first World Series title.

In 2011, Posey was injured in a violent home-plate collision. He

.336
Posey's MLB-leading batting average in 2012.

Birth Date: March 27, 1987
Birthplace: Leesburg, Georgia
Team: San Francisco Giants, 2009–
Height: 6 feet 1 (1.85 m)
Weight: 215 pounds (98 kg)
Breakthrough Season: Batted .305 as a rookie in 2010
Awards: College Baseball Player of the Year, 2008; NL Rookie of the Year, 2010; NL MVP, 2012; NL Comeback Player of the Year, 2012

missed more than 100 games of his second season with a broken leg and torn ankle ligaments. Posey returned and played even better the next year. In 2012, he led the NL in batting average and was named NL MVP. He also won the Comeback Player of the Year Award for overcoming his leg injury. And the Giants won the World Series again.

The Giants sometimes use Posey at first base. This helps offset the physical demands of being a full-time catcher. When behind the plate, Posey shows off a strong arm and quick release. These skills make him one of the toughest catchers to steal bases against.

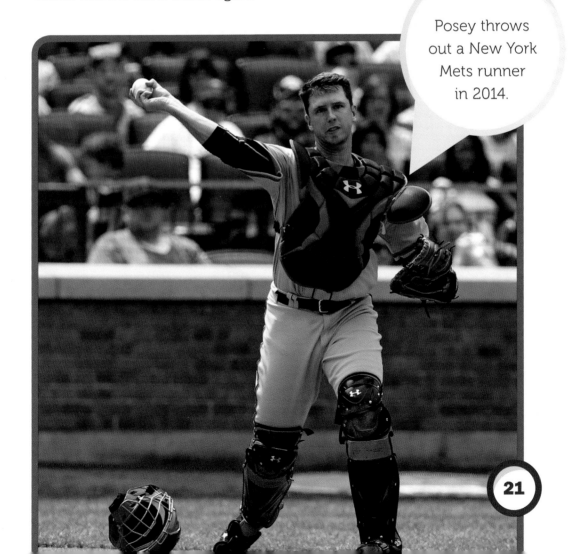

Posey throws out a New York Mets runner in 2014.

YASIEL PUIG MAKES INSTANT IMPACT IN THE UNITED STATES

Yasiel Puig grew up loving baseball. He played for the junior national team in Cuba when he was 17. Following the lead of players who came before him, Puig sought to reach the United States against his government's wishes. Puig made it to Mexico and on to the United States in 2012. He then signed with the Los Angeles Dodgers in 2012.

Puig watches his ball fly during a game against the Chicago Cubs in 2014.

4

Number of home runs Puig hit in his first five major league games.

Birth Date: December 7, 1990

Birthplace: Cienfuegos, Cuba

Team: Los Angeles Dodgers, 2013–

Height: 6 feet 3 (1.91 m)

Weight: 235 pounds (107 kg)

Breakthrough Season: Finished second in NL Rookie of the Year voting in 2013

Awards: NL Player of the Month, June 2013 and May 2014

Puig catches a fly ball in right field.

Puig immediately made it clear he was ready to play against the best.

Puig spent just 63 games with three Dodgers minor league teams. He rose quickly in late 2012 and early 2013. He batted well over .300 at each stop. Puig was called up by the Dodgers on June 3, 2013. That month, he was named NL Player of the Month.

Puig's power hitting makes each at-bat interesting. He provides excitement in the field as well. His powerful arm from right field makes him one of the best at stopping runners trying to advance on the bases.

MIKE TROUT OFFERS POWER AND SPEED IN ONE PACKAGE

Mike Trout grew up in New Jersey. He played football and basketball as a child, but he loved baseball. His father, Jeff Trout, was once drafted by the Minnesota Twins. Jeff helped coach Mike, and by high school, Mike was becoming a star. He set a high school state record for home runs in one season with 18.

After high school it was off to the minor leagues. Trout was the number one draft pick of the Los Angeles Angels of Anaheim in 2009. The Angels called him up in 2011. Trout was only 19 years old. In his first three full seasons the outfielder won one AL MVP award and was the runner-up twice.

Trout hits baseballs over the wall for home runs. When he is not hitting homers, he gets around the bases

with hits and steals. He led the AL in runs scored as a rookie in 2012. When in the outfield, he leaps above the wall to take home runs away from opposing batters. Trout also has great speed. This helps him chase down fly balls in the outfield.

49
Trout's MLB-leading stolen base total in 2012.

Birth Date: August 7, 1991
Birthplace: Vineland, New Jersey
Team: Los Angeles Angels of Anaheim, 2011–
Height: 6 feet 2 (1.88 m)
Weight: 230 pounds (104 kg)
Breakthrough Season: Second in MVP voting as a rookie in 2012
Awards: AL Rookie of the Year, 2012; AL MVP, 2014

Trout slides and steals third against the Boston Red Sox in 2013.

TROY TULOWITZKI SHINES AT BAT AND AT SHORTSTOP

Troy Tulowitzki was all-state in both baseball and basketball while growing up in California. But he was not considered a major pro prospect. Three years of baseball at Long Beach State changed that. The Colorado Rockies picked Tulowitzki seventh overall in the 2005 MLB Draft.

Tulowitzki quickly showed his value as a shortstop. In his first full season, Tulowitzki helped the Colorado Rockies make it to their first World Series in 2007.

Tulowitzki is big for a shortstop. But he moves quickly. Tulowitzki has great range and covers a lot of territory. His strong arm helps him make tough throws to first base look easy. His sure hands almost never misplay the ball. Playing excellent defense is a big part of playing shortstop. Tulowitzki won the Gold Glove as the NL's best defensive shortstop in 2010 and 2011.

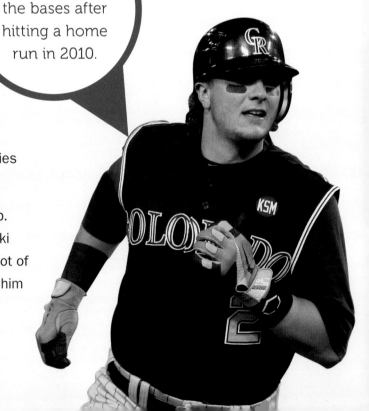

Tulowitzki circles the bases after hitting a home run in 2010.

A LOVE FOR THE GAME

Even when compared to other professional players, Tulowitzki is a baseball fanatic. Teammates and friends have to tell him to take a break sometimes. "I'll watch ESPN," Tulowitzki told *USA Today.* "I'll watch the MLB channel. I'll pick up the newspaper and read what's going on. I'll read the box scores. What can I say? I love the game."

105

Tulowitzki's career-high RBI total in 2011.

Birth Date: October 10, 1984

Birthplace: Santa Clara, California

Team: Colorado Rockies, 2006–

Height: 6 feet 3 (1.91 m)

Weight: 215 pounds (98 kg)

Breakthrough Season: Helped the Rockies to the World Series, led NL shortstops in most defensive statistics, and finished second in Rookie of the Year voting in 2007

Awards: NL Gold Glove, 2010 and 2011

Tulowitzki has been a defensive standout from the time he arrived in the major leagues.

FACT SHEET

- Major League Baseball is made up of 30 teams, 15 each from the American and National Leagues. Each league is split into East, Central, and West divisions of five teams each. Division champions and "wild cards," the teams with the best records among the non-champions, advance to league playoffs. The champions of each league's playoffs meet in the World Series each season. The first team to win four World Series games wins the championship.

- Each MLB team also has an organization of several minor league teams. Those teams play in leagues on different levels throughout the country. Often referred to as the "farm system," MLB teams use their minor leagues to train their future players. As players improve and gain experience, they move up in levels. There are two levels of rookie leagues where most players start their professional careers. From there, they go through two levels of Class A, then Double-A and Triple-A. A player can skip levels if his MLB team thinks he is ready to move up the ladder more quickly. However, many players never it make it out of the minor leagues.

- Wins and losses determine the order of standings for teams in each division. MLB has a tradition of using many other statistics to compare players in games, seasons, and entire careers. Batting average shows how often a player reaches base by a hit. A player who gets three hits for every 10 at-bats has a .300 average. Walks and certain other results are not counted as at-bats. Earned run average (ERA) shows how many earned runs a pitcher allows for each nine innings pitched. Runs that score because of errors by fielders are not counted as earned runs.

A pitcher who gives up three earned runs in nine innings has a 3.00 ERA. A pitcher who gives up one earned run in three innings also has a 3.00 ERA. Home runs is another category that gets a lot of attention. Most home runs occur when a player hits the ball over the outfield fence. But if a player hits a ball and can touch all four bases before the fielders tag him out, that is called an inside-the-park home run.

GLOSSARY

batting average
A three-digit percentage that shows how often a player reaches base by a hit.

contract
A written agreement committing a player to a team. It also specifies how much the player is paid.

earned run average (ERA)
The average number of earned runs, or runs scored that are not caused by a fielding error, a pitcher allows per nine innings.

error
Misplaying a ball in the field to allow a batter to reach base or a runner to advance.

home run
A hit that allows a player to safely circle all four bases.

minor leagues
A series of teams and leagues that develops players for the major leagues.

Most Valuable Player (MVP)
An award given to the top player in a season or event.

playoffs
Games played at the end of the season to decide a champion. When a team loses in the playoffs, its season is over.

rookie
A professional player in his first year.

runs batted in (RBI)
Hits, walks, or other results by a batter that allow his team to score a run.

FOR MORE INFORMATION

Books

Chandler, Matt. *Side-by-Side Baseball Stars: Comparing Pro Baseball's Greatest Players*. North Mankato, MN: Capstone Press, 2015.

Howell, Brian. *Playing Pro Baseball*. Minneapolis, MN: Lerner Publications, 2015.

Martin, Isabel. *Jackie Robinson*. North Mankato, MN: Pebble Books, 2015.

Websites

Baseball Hall of Fame
www.baseballhall.org

ESPN
www.espn.com

Major League Baseball
www.mlb.com

INDEX

About the Author

Tom Robinson is the author of more than three dozen books for children. He has written biographies and books about sports, history, and social issues. He lives in Clarks Summit, Pennsylvania.

READ MORE FROM 12-STORY LIBRARY

Every 12-Story Library book is available in many formats, including Amazon Kindle and Apple iBooks. For more information, visit your device's store or 12StoryLibrary.com.